The Blue wagon

Heather's treasure hunt

Karen R Sullivan

DEDICATION

This book is dedicated to the memory of my mother, who encouraged me to write stories as a child. And to my second mother, Marilyn, whose unconditional love and steadfast encouragement—including her belief that I should publish this book—have been a gift beyond measure. Her belief in me gave me the courage to share this story with the world.

You both have been a treasure in my life, and I deeply thank you.

Paperback ISBN: 978-1-968404-86-4
LCCN :2025918000

ACKNOWLEDGEMENT

First and foremost, I thank God for inspiring The Blue Wagon and guiding me throughout its creation. Every word, every illustration, and every quiet moment of reflection was a gift of grace.

To my second mom—thank you for encouraging me to publish this book. Your faith in me was like a quiet whisper of hope that grew louder with every step forward.

To my best friend Ardith and my cousin Robin—thank you for being among the very first to read The Blue Wagon. Your thoughtful feedback and warm encouragement helped me see the value of the story and trust that it deserved a place in the world.

To Teresa—I acknowledge you with gratitude for the inspiration you've given me along the way.

To Everly—thank you for reminding me what 8-year-olds are like. Your spark, curiosity, and genuine wonder helped me stay rooted in the heart of childhood.

To my sister Sandy—though we may not agree on everything, we agree that we're in each other's corners. Thank you for being part of my journey and for showing up with love when it mattered most.

To my dear friend Moe—thank you for being my sounding board, brainstorming partner, and ever-present source of clarity and creativity throughout this journey.

I hope that those who read this book receive the hope I poured into its pages. May it lift hearts, spark kindness, and bring joy. I've loved every moment of writing it, and it is my deepest wish that you'll find something to love in reading it too.

INTRODUCTION:

Heather loved collecting: shiny buttons, lost marbles, even cloud shapes in her scrapbook. But today she wanted something bigger—treasures that clinked and clunked."

Heather pulled her blue wagon down the street. Well, Heather was six, so she pulled it down the sidewalk. But the blue wagon was empty. She wanted to find treasures to put in it. So she walked down the sidewalk, pulling her blue wagon and looking for treasures.

She came across a large rock. It had crystals growing in it. "It was so pretty," she thought. "I will add that to my wagon." So she picked up the rock, which was pretty heavy—and for a six-year-old, she was pretty strong—so she picked it up and put it in her wagon.

She walked a little ways further and came across another rock. This time, it was round and white and had little swirly gray areas in it. She thought about it and thought, "I think that's marble." She had seen it before when she was in Brownies and they taught them about taking care of fishes.

In the bottom of the aquarium was marble, so this looked very much like it. So she picked up the round piece of marble and put it in her wagon—her beautiful blue wagon. So she had two treasures now.

As she kept going, she met Mr. Wiggledimp. She just loved his name, and she loved him. He was a very nice man. He asked her what she was doing today. She told him she was looking for treasures. He looked thoughtfully at her for a minute and went inside his house after telling her to stay there for a minute.

A minute later, he came out and he had a large piece of colored rock. It was a rainbow of colors.

"What a beautiful rock!" she exclaimed. He said, "I have had this rock for many, many years. When I was a boy, I painted it and it became my big pet rock. My children don't want to have this after..."

He thought for a minute. "...after I leave
my house. So," he said, "would you like it,
Heather?"
Her eyes grew big. "It's beautiful! Yes, I
would like it very much!"
"Well, it's yours then. Consider it my gift
to you on your treasure hunt."
He came down his sidewalk and walked
up to Heather and put it in her blue
wagon.
"I see you've got a couple of other
treasures," he said."Yes," she said.
He placed the rock in her wagon.
"Thank you, Mr. Wiggledimp. I have to go
now so that I can find more treasures."
He said, "Well, happy treasure hunting."

So she kept walking. She was almost to the end of the street, where she couldn't go any further, and she began to get a little tired. So she sat down in her wagon and rested and looked beside her at her treasures. She felt a sense of satisfaction.

"I have three treasures. My hunt has been very good," she thought.

Just then, she spotted something in the ground. It had holes in it and was very big. She thought, "That will make a nice treasure." So she dug around the dirt a little bit, trying not to get her dress very dirty. After all, she was a little girl.

Her mother expected a little dirt. But she dug around and got the rock and brought it out of the ground. She looked it over, and it was so full of holes that she thought, "I wonder if I really want this one?" But she thought, "Well, I bet no one else would want it, so I'll add it to my treasures."
She heard someone say once that one man's trash is another man's treasure. She thought that she heard that in school. So she took the rock and added it to her collection. She turned around and walked back down the street.

Mr. Wiggledimp was still sitting on his porch. She walked by and said, "Hello again, Mr. Wiggledimp. Do you want to see my newest treasure?"

"Why, certainly, Heather. Let's see what you have there."

He walked up to her wagon—her blue wagon—and looked inside. He was amazed.

"That rock is full of fossils!" he said.

"What's a fossil?" she asked.
"They are marks made into the rock from many, many years ago. Maybe even when there were dinosaurs."
Her eyes widened. "Wow, dinosaurs could have seen this rock?"
"Yes, indeed," he said.
"Well then, it is a real treasure—maybe even realer than my other treasures."
"Maybe so," he said. "But don't discount the other treasures. Just because one's older or more valuable doesn't make the other ones less valuable. Treasures are like that. It doesn't matter how important they are or how valuable they are—it only matters that they are valuable to you."

She nodded. "Okay then. I have four treasures. One of them maybe even stepped on by a dinosaur."
He laughed. "Maybe indeed," he said. "I have to go home now. It's dinner time. See you later, Mr. Wiggledimp."
"I will see you later too, Miss Heather."
She giggled. "I'm not a Miss," she said.He said, "Well, I believe you are, and I know some things."She nodded her head and began to leave toward home. She was getting tired again, so she sat down in her wagon and rested again.

"I wonder why I keep getting tired?" she thought to herself. "I wasn't tired when I started on my treasure hunt, but now I am growing very weary," she thought.
These were big rocks. They were very heavy to pull. She thought about it for a minute and decided, Maybe I'm getting tired because I'm pulling such a heavy load. She wondered about that thought. Could that be? Her rocks were dragging her down? She wasn't really sure, but it was strange that the way back was harder than the way there.

She finally arrived home and pulled her blue wagon up to the steps. She sat on the steps and looked at her treasures. This has been a very fun treasure hunt, she thought to herself. I have to go get Mama and show her my treasures. So she left her wagon at the bottom of the stairs and went in to get her mother. Her mother was in the kitchen making dinner, and she looked really tired. At least, that's what Heather thought. But she walked up to her.

"Mama, will you look at my treasures?"

"Not right now, Heather. You go get washed up for dinner."

Heather was a little disappointed, but she did as she was told and went and washed up for dinner.

I sure wish Mama would have looked at my treasures, she thought to herself. But maybe after dinner. She felt better at that thought and knew her mother would probably look at her treasures after dinner.

So she went into the kitchen and said, "Can I do anything to help, Mama?"

Her mother looked at her and said, "Can you get the plates?"

"Yes, of course," she said.

So she went to the kitchen cabinet and reached very high and got the plates down. She took them to the dining room and put them on the table at each person's place.

Then she walked into the living room and sat down, and then re-membered her wagon.

I better go see if my wagon is still there. Somebody might have stolen my treasures.

So she went outside, sat on the bottom step, and her treasures were still there. The sun was going down a little bit, and she decided she better hide them somewhere. So she pulled her wagon around to the back of the house and put it in the shed. Now it's safe, she thought.

She went back in. Her mother called them for dinner, so she waited through her dinner and waited and waited until her mother got up from the table. Heather got up from the table, and she went to her mother and said, "Will you look at my treasures now?"

"Let me wash the dishes first, then I will look at your treasures."

"Okay," she said. She had
learned a long time ago that
her mother was good for her
word, and if she said she
would look at her treasures,
then she would.
She went and watched some
television, came back about
half an hour later. Her mother
was sitting in a chair looking
very tired.

"Are you all right, Mama?"
Her mother looked at her and said,
"Yes, I'm just tired and worried."
"What's worry?" she asked her.
"It's just something that grown-ups do sometimes." After all, Mother didn't want to teach Heather about worry too soon.
"Okay," Heather said. "Will you look at my treasures now?"
"Yes, I will," her mother said. "Where are they?"
"I put them in my blue wagon in the shed."
"Okay, let's go look," her mother said.

So they went out the back door and to the shed. Her mother turned on the light and came into the shed. She looked at the four rocks and smiled. She had been six once; she knew how important treasures were to a six-year-old. "Aren't they wonderful?" Heather said.

"Where did you get these?" "I went on a treasure hunt today and I found them. And one of them came from Mr. Wiggledimp."

"Oh? Which one?" her mother said. She showed her the colored one, and her mother said, "Well, that's beautiful. Why did he give it to you?" "He said his children wouldn't want it, and when he moved, he couldn't take it. And since they didn't want it, he gave it to me."

"That's very kind of him," her mother said. "So tell me, how did you pull such a heavy load today?" "Well, I did get tired on the way back from my treasure hunt. I had to sit and rest twice because my wagon was getting heavy."

Her mother decided maybe six wasn't too young to learn about worry. So she started to tell Heather.

"Do you know why it got so tiring on the way back?" "I think it's because I was pulling a heavier load." Her mother looked at her. Could it be she already knew about worry? "Do you know, Heather, that that's exactly what worry is?" "What do you mean?" Heather said. "Sometimes grown-ups pull heavy loads too. Little girls pull heavy loads in wagons, and as you pick up more rocks, it gets harder and harder to pull the wagon. And sometimes grown-ups don't pull wagons, but they pull thoughts out of their heads. And those thoughts get heavy just like your rocks. And so sometimes they get tired too."

Heather thought about it. "Is that why you're so tired today, Mama?"

Oh, the wisdom of children. "Yes, sometimes that's why I get tired, Heather."

So they walked back into the house, hand in hand, not saying anything else. But Heather knew she had learned a very important lesson today—that pulling heavy things can be very tiring, even for grown-ups. She would never forget this lesson. And she didn't.

The End

www.ingramcontent.com/pod-product-compliance
Lightning Source LLC
Chambersburg PA
CBHW041411300726
48978CB00002B/58